Michael and the Cats

Also by Barbara Abercrombie and Mark Graham
CHARLIE ANDERSON

Also illustrated by Mark Graham
ROOMMATES by Kathryn O. Galbraith
ROOMMATES AND RACHEL by Kathryn O. Galbraith
HOME BY FIVE by Ruth Wallace-Brodeur

(Margaret K. McElderry Books)

Margaret K. McElderry Books
Macmillan Publishing Company
866 Third Avenue, New York, NY 10022

Maxwell Macmillan Canada, Inc.
1200 Eglinton Avenue East, Suite 200, Don Mills, Ontario M3C 3N1

Macmillan Publishing Company is part of the Maxwell Communication Group of Companies.
First edition   10   9   8   7   6   5   4   3   2   1
Printed in Hong Kong by South China Printing Company (1988) Ltd.
The text of this book is set in ITC Esprit Medium. The illustrations are rendered in oil paint.

Library of Congress Cataloging-in-Publication Data
Abercrombie, Barbara.
Michael and the cats / Barbara Abercrombie ; illustrated by Mark Graham. — 1st ed.
p.   cm.
Summary: On a visit to his aunt and uncle, Michael is delighted by their two cats but must
learn the proper way to make friends with them.
ISBN 0-689-50543-4
[1. Cats—Fiction.]   I. Graham, Mark, date, ill.   II. Title.
PZ7 A1614Mi 1993
[E]—dc20   91-23950

Michael and the Cats

Barbara Abercrombie · illustrated by Mark Graham

MARGARET K. McELDERRY BOOKS
New York

Maxwell Macmillan Canada
Toronto

Maxwell Macmillan International
New York Oxford Singapore Sydney

For Brooke and Gillan, with love
—B.A.

To William
—M.G.

Michael and his family came to visit his aunt and uncle, who had two cats. Michael had no pets. He had a baby brother instead.

Michael loved the cats right away. He tried to grab their soft fur. But the cats ran away and hid. He crawled under the bed after them. "Hi, cats! I'm your friend!"

"Don't scare the cats, Michael," said his mother. "Be gentle with them."

At dinner that night, Michael saved half his chocolate ripple ice cream for the cats.

"No ice cream for them," said his aunt. "It makes them sick."

The next morning was cold and windy. The cats meowed to go out. Michael tried to dress them up in his sweater and windbreaker to keep them warm. One cat chewed a button off the sweater. The other cat hissed at him. "Don't hurt the cats, Michael," said his uncle.

When they went to the store, Michael wanted to bring the cats. "Oh, no," said his aunt, "they hate to ride in the car."

Michael brought the cats into the bathroom
to keep him company while he took his bath.
"Cats are afraid of water," said his father.
"Don't get them wet."

When his mother tucked him into bed, Michael asked her where the cats slept. "In their own bed," she said, and kissed him good night.

Michael couldn't fall asleep. He kept thinking about the cats. He wanted to be friends with them. But how? He'd done all the things that would make him happy if he were a cat.

But he wasn't a cat. And the cats weren't little boys, he thought. The cats were cats. Maybe they liked other things.

For the next few days, Michael watched the cats carefully. When they scratched at the cupboard, he fed them their own food.

When they finished eating and meowed to go out, he opened the back door for them.

After lunch the cats always sunned themselves on the back porch. "Shh," Michael would say to his baby brother. "The cats are resting."

Every day Michael watched the cats. When he played Frisbee with his uncle, the cats climbed up in a tree and watched Michael.

Before he went to bed on the last night of his visit, his aunt read to him. The cats were dozing in front of the fireplace. Michael stretched out next to them. He wanted to hug them, but instead he stroked their heads gently.

In the middle of the night Michael suddenly woke up. Something had landed on his bed.

The cats were sitting next to his feet. "Hi, cats," he whispered.

They curled up against him. They felt warm and soft and friendly. Michael could hear them purring.